ONCE UPON A TIME
THERE LIVED A
TERRIBLE
DRAGON.

'Happily
Ever After'

...said the last page in
Jill's huge book.

But Jill noticed that not
everyone at the end of the
story looked so happy...

DOG

AND ✳ THEY

'Why are you sad, Dragon?' asked Jill.

'The King HATES me' said Dragon, his pathetic eyes looking up at her from the page. 'All I can do is burn, scorch, singe, char and barbeque everything in the Kingdom!'

'Don't worry, Dragon. You can come and live with me!' exclaimed Jill.

'I'm going to teach you how to do all my favourite things' said Jill to Dragon.

Jill taught Dragon all about
flower arr a n g i n g

Jill taught Dragon
about fashion...

Jill taught
Dragon how to play
the trumpet...

And finally Jill
taught Dragon
how to host a
tea party.

Dragon looked sadder than ever.
'I don't belong anywhere! All I do is
burn with my fire-y breath' he said.

Something at the tea table had
caught Jill's eye and she exclaimed
'I have an idea, Dragon!'

The next morning...

Armed with a fork, Jill jumped
onto Dragon's back and they
flew into the huge book.

Angry Knights greeted Jill and Dragon on the page. Jill feeling brave, jumped off Dragon, and shouted

'Take us to the King!'

TOAST

PORTRAIT

TO

THE

KING

The King took the toast from the Knights.

He nibbled a corner,

then a second corner

and then a third.

After a long pause his face
lit up and with a huge grin
he proclaimed
'This toast is truly
fit for a King!'

But wait!
Dragon was not finished yet!
Jill pulled out more slices of bread and
Dragon created even more intricate and
wonderful designs. As Dragon toasted
bread, day turned into night.

The fire from Dragon's breath sent colourful sparks into the air, which lit up the sky like fireworks. The King bowed before Dragon and said 'Dragon, you belong here. Come and live in my Castle, and make me toast.'

FOR ❋ EVERYONE

EVER ❋ AFTER

THE ❋ END

'We ALL have a happy ending now!' said Jill to her dog, as they read the last page in her book once more.